To my parents, who never told me
my dreams were nonsense

Library of Congress Cataloging-in-Publication data is on file with the publisher.

First published in 2015 by Macmillan Children's Books,
an imprint of Pan Macmillan, a division of Macmillan Publishers International Limited.
Text and illustrations copyright © Gemma Merino
Published in 2016 by Albert Whitman & Company
ISBN 978-0-8075-1298-2

Printed in China
10 9 8 7 6 5 4 3 2 WKT 20 19 18 17 16

For more information about Albert Whitman & Company,
visit our web site at www.albertwhitman.com.

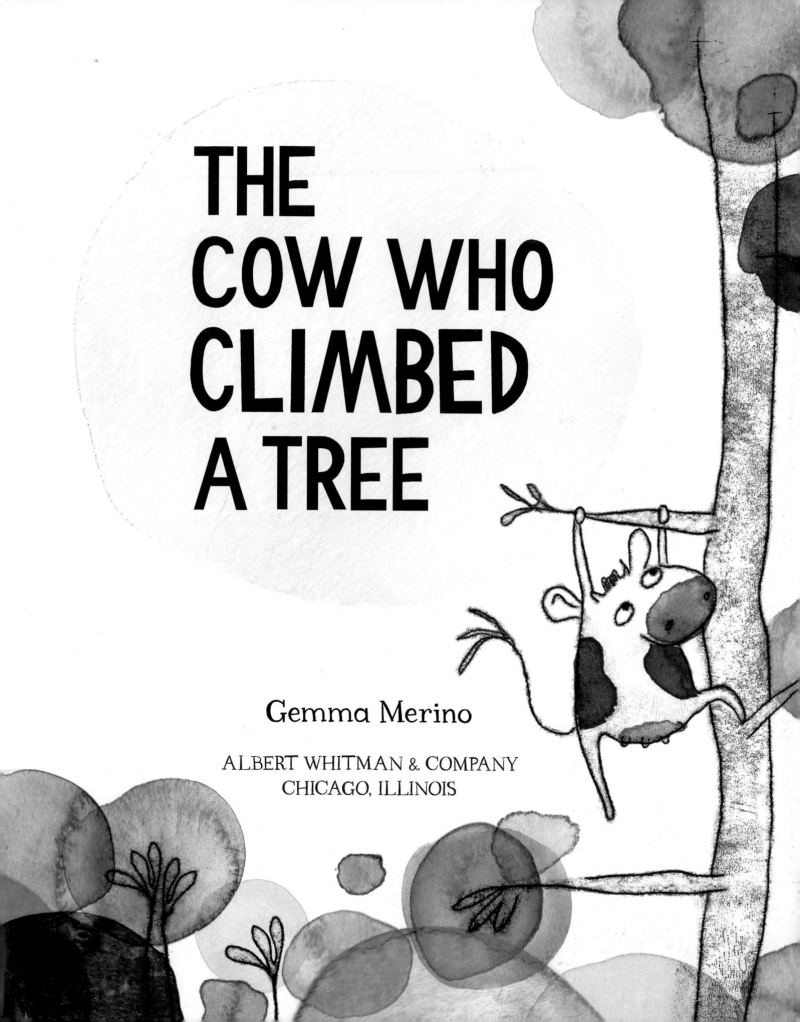

THE COW WHO CLIMBED A TREE

Gemma Merino

ALBERT WHITMAN & COMPANY
CHICAGO, ILLINOIS

Tina was a very curious cow.
She had a thirst for discovery.

Her mind was full of wonderful things,
all of which her sisters found very silly.

"IMPOSSIBLE!"
"RIDICULOUS!"
"NONSENSE!"
they would say every time
she told them her
amazing ideas.

Her sisters were only
interested in one thing:
fresh and juicy grass.

One day when Tina was exploring the woods,

she decided to try something new.

She began
to climb
a tree.

Up and up
she went.

When she got to the top,
Tina couldn't believe her eyes...

Unlike the fierce dragons
she had seen in her books,
this one was friendly...

and vegetarian.

All afternoon they talked
about wonderful dreams
and incredible stories.

Tina couldn't wait to tell
her sisters about her new friend.

But her sisters were NOT impressed.

"Dragons don't exist."

"Cows can't climb trees."

"IMPOSSIBLE! RIDICULOUS!
NONSENSE!" they said.

And with that they went to bed.

But the next morning,

Tina was nowhere
to be seen.

Her sisters found a note.

Well, that was it!

Tina's nonsense had gone too far.

The sisters decided to go and find her and bring her home.

For the first time, they ventured beyond the farm and into the woods.

They had never imagined
it would be so beautiful...

And then they came across something very strange.

"IMPOSSIBLE!" they said.

But the first sister
began to climb, and
one after another,
up they went.

The world beyond the fields was extraordinary.

But where was Tina?
Suddenly the sisters looked up...

It was IMPOSSIBLE.
It was RIDICULOUS.
It was NONSENSE.

But it was TRUE!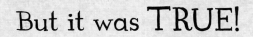

Tina was FLYING!

And when she asked her sisters to join her,
they said something they had never said before...

YES, WHY NOT?

And after that, they just couldn't
wait to see what else was possible.